"Mole!" cried Shrew. "I'm going to go to the big egg hunt. Do you want to come with me?"

"Egg hunt?" said Mole. He paused. He wasn't fond of hunting. Besides, why would anyone want to hunt eggs?

"Yes," said Shrew. "The mayor says that there are eggs hidden all over town!"

Oh, dear, thought Mole. Eggs *hiding* all over town! What could they be up to? Suddenly he gasped. What if they were *alien* eggs? An egg-vasion! No wonder Shrew was joining the hunt!

"I'll be there as fast as I can!" he replied.

To Gumpa, with love
—J. F. K.

For Alex and Graham
—J. B.

Text copyright © 1997 by Jackie French Koller.
Illustrations copyright © 1997 by John Beder.
All rights reserved under International and Pan-American Copyright Conventions.
Published in the United States by Random House, Inc., New York, and
simultaneously in Canada by Random House of Canada Limited, Toronto.

http://www.randomhouse.com/

Library of Congress Cataloging-in-Publication Data

Koller, Jackie French. Mole and Shrew all year through / by Jackie French Koller ;
illustrated by John Beder. p. cm. "A stepping stone book." Summary: In their
own original way, best friends Mole and Shrew celebrate five holidays throughout
the year.

ISBN 0-679-88666-4 (pbk.) — ISBN 0-679-98666-9 (lib. bdg.)

[1. Moles (Animals)—Fiction. 2. Shrews—Fiction. 3. Holidays—Fiction.
4. Friendship—Fiction.] I. Beder, John, ill. II. Title.
PZ7.K833Moj 1997 [E]—dc21 97–2133

Printed in the United States of America 10 9 8 7 6 5 4 3 2 1

MOLE AND SHREW
All Year Through

BY JACKIE FRENCH KOLLER

ILLUSTRATED BY JOHN BEDER

A STEPPING STONE BOOK

RANDOM HOUSE 🏠 NEW YORK

❧ Contents ☙

A NEW YEAR'S TALE   7
A Fresh Start

AN EASTER TALE   27
The Egg-vasion!

A FOURTH OF JULY TALE   41
Picnics and Parades

A THANKSGIVING TALE   57
Nothing to Be Thankful For

A CHRISTMAS TALE   69
The Good Friends' Fur Tree

A
NEW YEAR'S
TALE

A Fresh Start

Chapter One ✒

Mole sat in his favorite armchair. His feet were up on a hassock and his favorite book rested on his plump middle. More books overflowed from the shelves behind him, making a cozy clutter on the floor. A fire crackled in the fireplace. Fluffy white snowflakes drifted past the window.

"Ahhh," sighed Mole. "What a pleasant way to spend a cold winter's day."

Just then the telephone rang.

Brrrinng, it clattered, *brrrinng*, *brrrinng*, *brrrinng!*

"Oh, *brrrinng, brrrinng* yourself," Mole muttered. He put his book aside and heaved himself out of his chair.

"Good day," he said into the phone.

"Good day to you, too," answered the cheery voice of Mole's best friend, Shrew. "Do you know what day it is, Mole?"

Mole thought hard. Yesterday was Monday and tomorrow was Wednesday, so today must be...

"Tuesday!" he announced proudly.

"Well, yes," said Shrew. "It *is* Tuesday, but it's also something else, Mole. It's New Year's Eve!"

"It is?" Mole glanced up at his calendar. Indeed, Tuesday was the very last day on the very last page of the year! "Why, you're right, Shrew," he said. "I must have lost track of the days."

"You can't lose track of New Year's

Eve!" cried Shrew. "We have to celebrate!"

Mole's heart did a happy flippity-flip. He loved celebrations!

"I think New Year's Eve is the best night of the whole year," Shrew went on. "It's a chance for everyone to make a fresh start."

"Mmm," Mole murmured. He licked his lips at the thought of a fresh tart. Mole loved tarts more than almost anything else. "That sounds like a wonderful way to celebrate, Shrew," he said.

"Oh, I hoped you would say that," said Shrew. "Why don't you come over this evening? We'll both make a fresh start together."

"Certainly," said Mole. "Shall I bring anything?"

"Just your resolutions," said Shrew. "See you then!"

Click went the phone in Mole's ear. He held it out in front of him and stared at it. *Resolutions?* What were resolutions? Mole shrugged and hung up the phone.

"Must be something you put in tarts," he muttered.

Mole had never tasted resolution tarts, but if Shrew was going to make them, he knew they would be good. Mole closed his eyes. He pictured the fresh tarts coming out of the oven all steamy and golden.

"Mmm," he said to himself. "Maybe Shrew will serve them with whipped cream on top." He licked his lips once more, then went over to his cupboard. "Now to find some resolutions," said Mole.

He read the labels on all the boxes and jars inside. No resolutions. He checked his refrigerator. No resolutions there either.

Mole looked out the window at the snow and sighed.

"I guess I'll have to go to the store," he said.

Chapter Two

Mole put on his scarf and his boots. With a last, longing look at the crackling fire, he stepped out into the storm.

Wind tugged at Mole's scarf and whistled past his ears. Snowflakes landed on his eyelashes and stuck to his whiskers. But Mole trudged on, warming himself on the inside with thoughts of fresh tarts, hot from the oven.

At last Mole pushed through the door of the grocery store. He shook a cap of snow from his head.

"Why, hello there," said Badger, the storekeeper. "What brings you out on such a day?"

"Tarts," said Mole.

"What kind of tarts?" asked Badger.

"New Year's Eve tarts, of course," said Mole. "Everyone makes tarts on New Year's Eve."

Badger looked surprised. "Really?" he said. "I didn't know that."

Mole leaned in closer. "To be honest," he said, "neither did I. But Shrew says it's so, so it must be."

"Indeed," said Badger with a slow, thoughtful nod. "Shrew is a most truthful creature."

"You might think about making some

tarts yourself," said Mole. "You wouldn't want to be left out."

"No, indeed," Badger agreed. "No one likes to be left out."

Mole nodded, then hurried back to the fruit department.

"I do love berry tarts," he said to himself. He gazed longingly at the baskets of plump berries. "I hope resolutions are a type of berry."

Mole read the names on all the baskets. There were many kinds of berries: blueberries, blackberries, raspberries, gooseberries, huckleberries, cranberries, elderberries, strawberries, and *even* some berries called serviceberries. But there were no resolution berries.

An old gopher in a floppy, flowered hat was thumping the melons nearby.

"Pardon me," said Mole. "Do you think

a serviceberry might be something like a resolution?"

The gopher looked at him oddly.

"What are you talking about?" she asked.

"Berries," said Mole. "I asked if you thought a serviceberry and a resolution might be similar."

The gopher shook her head. "Hmm," she muttered. "I'm befuddled."

Mole reached out his hand.

"Pleased to meet you, Ms. Fuddled," he said. "I'm Mole. Now about those berries…"

But the gopher was already moving quickly away down the aisle.

Mole shrugged and went back to examining the fruit.

"Perhaps a resolution is some other type of fruit," he said hopefully.

Mole read the labels in front of all the other fruits. There were oranges, apples, and pears, mangos, melons, and bananas, and pineapples. There was even a fuzzy little brown thing called a kiwi.

A lizard with snow-speckled glasses came up. He began sniffing the bananas.

"Pardon me," said Mole. He held up a kiwi. "Does this look anything like a resolution to you?"

The lizard squinted at the kiwi, then sniffed it.

"A *what*?" he asked.

"A resolution," said Mole. "You see, I'm making resolution tarts and I want to find some nice ripe resolutions."

The lizard wrinkled his nose.

"I'm befuddled," he said.

"Really?" said Mole, sticking out his hand once more. "Pleased to meet you.

Are you by any chance related to the B. Fuddled in the floppy hat?"

The lizard frowned and said nothing more. He tucked his bananas under his arm and hurried away.

Mole sighed.

"Perhaps I'd better ask Badger," he said. He walked back up to the front of the store.

Chapter Three ⚬

"Pardon me, Badger," said Mole. "I was wondering if you had any resolutions."

"Oh, certainly," said Badger. "I'm going to try and lose five pounds. I'm going to stop biting my nails. And I'm going to give more money to the poor."

Mole listened politely. He wondered why Badger was planning on making so many changes in his life. More to the point, he wondered why Badger had suddenly begun telling him about them.

"That's all very good of you," said Mole when Badger was through speaking. "But can you answer my question now?"

"What question was that?" asked Badger.

"I wondered what kind of fruit a resolution is," said Mole. "And I wondered whether or not you have any."

Badger stared at Mole a long moment. "I think you must be befuddled," he said at last.

"Oh, no, I'm not," said Mole. "I can see how you might make that mistake, though. Several members of the Fuddled family do seem to be shopping here today. But I can promise you that I'm not one of them. I'm Mole. M-o-l-e, Mole."

Badger shook his head slowly. "Mole," he said, "why don't you start at the beginning? Tell me why you came to my store this morning."

"Okay," said Mole. "Shrew said we were going to make tarts, because it's New Year's Eve, you know. So I asked what I should bring and she said to just bring resolutions."

Badger smiled. "Ah, now I see," he said. "Resolutions are not ingredients for tarts, Mole. Resolutions are ideas about how you can make yourself better in the New Year. Shrew wants you to bring a list of your ideas."

"Oh," said Mole. "Is that all?"

"That's all," said Badger.

"Well," said Mole. "That sounds simple. But...I think I'll take a basket of those raspberries anyway—just in case."

Mole hurried home and sank into his chair again. He worked on his resolutions all afternoon.

Chapter
Four

Just as Mole was writing down his last resolution, the clock bonged six times.

"Oh! Time to go," he cried.

He took his resolutions and his raspberries and hurried off to Shrew's house.

"Happy New Year, Mole!" cried Shrew when she opened her door.

"Happy New Year!" Mole replied.

He handed Shrew the basket of raspberries.

"Why, thank you, Mole," said Shrew. "What a thoughtful gift. Have you brought your resolutions?"

"Right here," said Mole, holding up his list.

Shrew poured two cups of steaming

tea and set them on the tea table. She and Mole sat down on the sofa.

"You read yours first, Mole," said Shrew, "then I'll read mine."

Mole took a sip of tea, then cleared his throat.

"These are my resolutions for the New Year," he read. "I'm going to put a Band-Aid on whenever I cut myself. I'm going to drink chicken soup when I have the flu. I'm going to take vitamin C when I have a cold. I'm going to…"

Shrew's eyes widened as Mole read one resolution after another.

"Well, Mole," she said when he was through, "those are very…*interesting* resolutions."

Mole beamed. "They're all the ways I could think of to make myself better in the New Year," he said.

Shrew smiled slowly. "Ah," she said, "and very good ways they are, Mole."

"Did you come up with any different ones?" Mole asked.

Shrew quietly folded her list and

tucked it away in her apron pocket.

"No, Mole," she said. "I think you've just about covered them all."

"Good," said Mole. "Does that mean we can make the tarts now?"

"The tarts?" asked Shrew.

"Yes," said Mole. "Remember you said we would each celebrate the New Year by making a fresh tart?"

Shrew's smile grew.

"Of course I remember," she said. "What better way to begin the New Year than to make a fresh tart with an old friend?"

"What better way, indeed?" Mole grinned.

Shrew picked up the basket of raspberries. "Let's get cooking!" she cried.

An
Easter
Tale

The Egg-vasion!

Chapter One ✺

The sky was clear and blue. The air smelled fresh and new. Sunshine warmed Mole's neck as he swept last fall's moldy leaves from his garden. He bent to admire a bright daffodil.

"How I love spring," he sang to himself.

Just then the telephone rang. Mole hurried inside to answer it.

"Mole!" cried Shrew. "I'm going to go to the big egg hunt. Do you want to come with me?"

"Egg hunt?" said Mole. He paused. He wasn't fond of hunting. Besides, why would anyone want to hunt eggs?

"Yes," said Shrew. "The mayor says that there are eggs hidden all over town!"

Oh, dear, thought Mole. Eggs *hiding* all over town! What could they be up to? Suddenly he gasped. What if they were *alien* eggs? An egg-vasion! No wonder Shrew was joining the hunt!

"I'll be there as fast as I can!" he replied.

"Wonderful!" said Shrew. "I'll meet you at the park."

Mole hung up the phone. He peered worriedly at himself in his front hall mirror.

"How brave Shrew is," he told himself. "She doesn't sound a bit scared. I must be

brave, too. Even if they are *alien* eggs." A shiver ran up his back.

Mole went up to his attic to search for something to hunt with. He found a bow and some foam-rubber arrows.

"Perhaps these will do," he said.

He tried shooting one at his foot. The arrow felt like a soft little tap on his toe.

"I guess not," said Mole.

Next he found a plastic gun that shot red plastic balls. He tried that, too. The ball felt like a gentle poke.

"Not this either," said Mole.

Then he tried a slingshot with a small stone.

"Ouch!" he cried when the stone stung his toe like an angry bee. "This should do."

Next he wondered what to wear.

"Maybe an alien egg is a water

creature," he said. "I should wear my wading boots, just in case."

Mole pulled on his long rubber boots.

Next he dug out a bright orange sweater. He didn't want other hunters to hunt *him* by mistake.

"I guess I'm ready," he said with a sigh.

Mole plopped his fishing hat on his head and set off for the park.

Chapter Two

Mole walked cautiously down the lane. He kept a sharp eye out for egg tracks. As he neared Fox's house he heard a strange sound.

Ping! Ping!

Suddenly, a small white thing came hurtling through the air straight at him!

"An egg!" cried Mole. He dove for cover behind a bush and lay there trembling.

"Mole?"

Mole peered up into Fox's large brown eyes.

"I thought that was you," said Fox. "What's wrong?"

"Eggs," whispered Mole. "They're everywhere!"

"Really?" said Fox. "I thought most of them were down around the park. I was planning to join the hunt later."

Mole took a deep breath. How brave Fox was! If Shrew *and* Fox could be brave, he could be brave, too. He stood up and walked around the bush.

"Look!" he cried, pointing to a small white thing on the ground. "There's one right there!"

Fox shook her head. "That's not an egg, Mole," she said, bending to pick up the white thing. "It's a Ping-Pong ball. Rabbit and I were playing Ping-Pong in my backyard. Would you like to play, too?"

"Oh." Mole put his hand to his thumping heart. "No, thank you, Fox. I promised Shrew I'd join her at the egg hunt."

"Good for you," said Fox. "I hope you find lots!"

"We will," said Mole bravely. "We won't rest until we've found them all!"

Chapter Three 🐾

At last Mole reached the park. His heart was still thumping and he was a bit out of breath from hurrying. The park was full of hunters. They were all crawling on their

knees and poking in the bushes. Finally
Mole spied Shrew. He waved his slingshot.
"Mole reporting for duty!" he cried.
"Reporting for *what*?" asked Shrew.

"For duty," said Mole. "We'll get every last one of those eggs. Don't you worry."

Shrew started to smile. Then she started to giggle. Then she started to laugh.

"What's so funny?" asked Mole.

"Oh, Mole," said Shrew. "That's not how you hunt eggs!"

Mole began to feel foolish. He hated being laughed at. He lowered his slingshot and looked around. All of his neighbors were staring.

Shrew stopped laughing.

"I'm sorry, Mole," she said gently. "I...I wasn't laughing at you."

Mole looked at her forlornly. "It sounded like laughing," he said.

"It...was laughing," said Shrew. "But I was laughing...at myself. Yes, that's it."

"But why would you laugh at

yourself, Shrew?" asked Mole.

"For being so silly," said Shrew. "For forgetting to tell you."

"Forgetting to tell me what?" asked Mole.

"Forgetting to tell you that you can't hunt eggs with a slingshot."

"You can't?" asked Mole.

"Oh, no," said Shrew. "Their shells would break."

"Yuck." Mole wrinkled up his nose. "That *would* be messy. I'll run right home and get my butterfly net."

"No, Mole," said Shrew. "You don't use a butterfly net either. You use one of these."

Shrew handed Mole a brightly colored basket.

"A basket?" said Mole.

"Yes," said Shrew. "You see..." She

leaned in close to Mole's ear. "Eggs like to sleep during the day."

"They do?" said Mole.

"Shhh!" Shrew touched a finger to her lips. "Yes," she said, "and if you're very quiet, you can sneak right up and put them in your basket."

"Oh," said Mole, "that *is* a relief." He wiggled his sore toe. "Slingshots make me nervous."

"Me, too," said Shrew.

She took Mole's slingshot and tucked it into her apron pocket. Then she picked up her basket and slipped her arm through Mole's.

"On with the hunt!" she called to everyone.

"Shhh!" Mole reminded her. "Don't wake the eggs."

A
FOURTH OF JULY
TALE

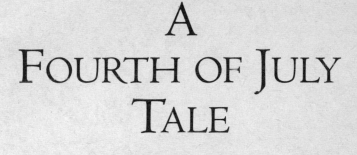

Picnics and Parades

Chapter
One ♪

Shrew hummed softly as she snipped her roses. The summer sun was high and hot. Bees droned and grasshoppers buzzed.

"Hello, Shrew," called Mole as he came down the lane. "How are you this fine day?"

"I'm well, thank you, Mole," said Shrew. "Would you like to help me cut roses?"

"Why?" asked Mole. "They look so pretty right there by the fence."

"I'm going to make a float," said

Shrew. "Would you like to help me?"

"I love floats," said Mole. He licked his lips. "Especially root-beer ones. But I never tasted a rose float. Are we going to have them on our Fourth of July picnic?"

"I don't mean the kind of float you drink," said Shrew with a laugh. "I mean the kind you have in a parade. Do you know what I've been thinking, Mole?"

Mole scratched his head. "No," he said. "Should I? Because I don't know how I could, unless you tell me."

Shrew giggled. "I *am* going to tell you," she said. "I've been thinking we should have a Fourth of July parade this year, instead of a picnic."

Mole thought about Shrew's idea. A picnic involved eating and drinking and sitting, three of Mole's favorite pastimes. A parade involved marching...and marching…and marching—under the hot, hot sun.

"I think I like picnics better than parades," he said.

"I like picnics, too," said Shrew. "But parades are the best part of the Fourth of July."

"No," said Mole. "Picnics are the best part of the Fourth of July."

"Everyone else would rather have a parade," said Shrew.

"I think they'd rather picnic," said Mole.

"*Parade,*" said Shrew in a loud voice.

"*Picnic,*" said Mole in a louder voice.

"Stop being so stubborn," said Shrew. "We *always* do things your way."

"No, we don't," said Mole. "We always do things your way, because you're so *bossy.*"

"Bossy!" Shrew stomped her foot. "Fine!" she said. "Have your boring old picnic, then. I don't need you to have a parade. I don't need *anyone* to have a parade. I can have a parade all by myself!"

"I don't need anyone either," said Mole. He stomped his foot, too. "I can have a picnic all by *myself!*"

Chapter Two 🐀

Mole got out his picnic basket and lined it with a red checked cloth. He made a tall stack of peanut butter and banana sandwiches and put them in. He added some cheese and crackers, some carrots and celery, and a big chunk of watermelon. For dessert, he baked cherry tarts and fudge brownies. Then he poured fresh lemonade with sugar into a jar.

"Yum." Mole licked his lips as he loaded the last of the goodies into his basket. "Shrew doesn't know what she's missing."

Off he went, down the lane toward the park. He swung his basket and whistled a happy tune.

Shrew was whistling, too, as she put the finishing touches on her float. It was a great big teapot, all made of roses. When it was done, she went up to her attic and dug out her old band uniform. Then she got out her drum. She was all ready to go when she spied her cousin Vole's tuba.

"Oh, how I love the sound of a tuba," she said. "I wonder if I can manage both."

She pulled the tuba strap over her head
and pushed her drum off to one side.
"Sure, I can!" she said. "What fun! And
won't Mole be jealous!"

Off she went—OOM*pah*, *tada-dum*,
OOM*pah* *tada-dum!*—pulling her float
behind her.

٭

Mole spread his picnic cloth under a nice,
cool tree and sat down. He took out his
sandwiches, snacks, dessert, and lemonade.
He looked around. It was very quiet.

"Nice and peaceful," he said. "Just the
way I like it."

Mole ate a peanut butter and banana
sandwich and some cheese. Then he ate
some watermelon and a tart. Then he ate
another sandwich and some more
watermelon. Now his tummy was full.

Mole sighed. "Last Fourth of July,

Shrew and I played hide-and-seek," he said. He stood up. "No problem," he told himself. "I'll just play hide-and-seek by myself."

Mole walked around the tree and

crouched against the trunk.

"Come and find yourself!" he called.

He waited a few moments, then answered, "Well, here you are!"

He frowned. It wasn't the same. He didn't get that shivery feeling he always got when he was hiding and Shrew was looking for him.

"Who cares about hiding anyway?" he said. He sat back down and drank some more lemonade.

❧

OOMpah, tada-dum, OOMpah tada-dum!

Shrew stopped and mopped her brow. It was hard work playing her instruments *and* pulling her float. And hot, too. She began to wish for a sip of lemonade.

She remembered last Fourth of July. Mole had brought a whole jar of fresh lemonade to their picnic.

"Oh, who cares about lemonade anyway?" she said. She knelt beside a brook and took a sip of water, then started off again.

OOMpah, *tada-dum*, OOMpah *tada-dum!*

Chapter
Three ↳

OOMpah, tada-dum, OOMpah tada-dum!

Mole looked up. Over the hill came Shrew and her parade. My, she looked as if she was having fun! What a lovely float! And a *tuba!*

Mole couldn't help feeling a little bit jealous. But...he went right on sitting.

OOMpah, tada-dum, OOMpah tada-dum!

Shrew looked over at Mole as she marched by. What a nice cool spot he had chosen for his picnic. And look at all that *food*. And fresh lemonade, too!

Shrew couldn't help feeling that she was missing something. But...she went right on marching.

As soon as Shrew passed by, Mole

began to have doubts.

"Maybe I *should* have been in Shrew's parade," he said.

As soon as Mole was out of sight, Shrew began to have doubts.

"Maybe I *should* have gone on Mole's picnic," she said to herself.

Suddenly Mole had a thought. He jumped up.

Suddenly Shrew had a thought. She spun around.

"Shrew!" cried Mole.

"Mole!" cried Shrew.

"Why don't we have a parade *and* a picnic!" they cried at once.

Mole and Shrew started to laugh. Shrew lifted the tuba over her head and handed it to Mole.

OOMpah, tada-dum, OOMpah tada-dum! they went. *OOMpah, tada-dum,*

OOMpah tada-dum! all around the park.

Soon others began to join in. Rabbit came running with his trumpet. Fox hurried up with her fife. Hedgehog brought up the rear with her clarinet, and Squirrel led them all with his twirling baton.

Through the forest they went, around the lake, and right back to the park. There they had sandwiches, watermelon, tarts, and lemonade. Then they played hide-and-seek.

❦

"You know what I've been thinking?" said Shrew to Mole as they sat watching the fireworks that evening.

"No," said Mole. "Should I?"

"Yes," said Shrew, "you should, because I've been thinking that the best part of the Fourth of July isn't having a parade *or* a picnic. It's having friends like you to share them with."

Mole smiled. "You know, Shrew," he said, "that's just what *I've* been thinking."

A
THANKSGIVING
TALE

Nothing to Be Thankful For

Chapter One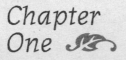

It was Thanksgiving Day. The trees outside Shrew's windows were bare and gray. Crisp leaves scurried across her yard, chased by a chilly breeze. The smell of wood smoke drifted in the air.

Shrew was busy getting ready. Hedgehog, Fox, and Mole were coming for Thanksgiving dinner. A pumpkin pie baked in the oven, perfuming the air with its spicy scent. Shrew mopped her kitchen and dusted her living room. She covered her table with a fresh cloth and tossed the old one into the washer. Then she set out her best china, lit a fire in the fireplace, and put on some soft holiday music.

At last everything was done.

"My, my," said Shrew as she smiled upon the cozy scene before her. "How I love Thanksgiving!"

Bong, bong, bong, bong went Shrew's clock.

"Oh, dear," she cried. "My guests will be here any minute!"

She hurried upstairs to her room to get dressed for dinner.

Chapter Two ﹏

Shrew took her best dress out of

the closet. Suddenly a loud sound came from downstairs. *Thumpety-gablunkety-GRONK!*

"My washing machine!" Shrew cried.

She dashed downstairs to see what was the matter.

"Oh, no!" Water was bubbling out of the top! Soapsuds were oozing down the sides!

Shrew ran to get her mop. By the time she returned, the flood was halfway across her kitchen and heading for the living room! She swished this way and that, this way and that. Then—*Crrr...aack!*—the mop handle broke.

"What next?" moaned Shrew.

Just then she caught a whiff of a strange, sharp smell. She turned to see a plume of smoke rising from her oven.

"My pie!" she shrieked.

She ran for the oven when suddenly—
whoosh!—her feet slipped on the sudsy
floor. She flipped up in the air and landed
in the middle of her table. *Crrr...unk!* It
cracked in half. Shrew and everything else
fell to the floor.

"Ooof," Shrew moaned.

She got to her feet again and sloshed
over to the oven. She pulled open the

door and smoke billowed out.

"Oh, no!" she cried, grabbing for the pie.

"Yeow!"

Shrew dropped the hot pie on the open door. In her haste, she had forgotten to use a mitt! She ran to the sink and turned on the tap. She plunged her hand into the cold water. How it hurt!

Ding, dong went Shrew's doorbell.

"My guests!" she cried. "And I'm not even dressed!"

Shrew dashed back upstairs. She yanked and pulled her dress over her head.

R-R-R-Rip! Off popped a button.

Shrew sank down into a heap. Tears rolled down her cheeks.

Chapter Three 🐍

Shrew slowly pulled her front door open. There stood Mole.

"Shrew?" he cried. "What's wrong? I was beginning to think no one was home."

"*Everything* is wrong," said Shrew with a sniff. "I'm canceling Thanksgiving, Mole."

"Canceling Thanksgiving!" cried Mole. "But...why?"

Shrew turned and stared at her ruined little house.

"Because," she said sadly, "I have nothing to be thankful for."

Mole stepped inside and took a long look around.

"Tell me what happened," he said.

Mole found a sock stuck in Shrew's washer. He pulled it out and dried up the rest of the flood with a towel.

"Now what?" he asked.

Shrew showed him the pie.

"Just the way I like it," he said.

"Charcoal makes your teeth white. What else?"

Shrew pointed to the table.

"We'll have a picnic in front of the fireplace," said Mole. "What could be cozier?"

Shrew started to smile.

"Next?" asked Mole.

Shrew held out her throbbing hand. Mole found some soothing cream and rubbed it on. Then he wrapped her hand in gauze.

"Is that it?" he asked.

"One more thing," said Shrew. She turned around and showed him the back of her dress.

Mole pulled a safety pin out of his vest pocket.

"Mother Mole told me to always carry a safety pin," he said as he pinned the top of Shrew's dress. "There. What a lovely dress, Shrew."

Ding, dong went Shrew's doorbell again.

"That must be Fox and Hedgehog,"

said Mole. "Shall I tell them that Thanksgiving is canceled?"

Shrew smiled. "No, Mole," she said. "I've remembered that I *do* have something to be thankful for after all. I have you."

Mole grinned. "Oh!" he said. "That reminds me."

He pulled two round sticks out of his back pocket and handed them to Shrew.

"What are these?" she asked.

"Drumsticks," said Mole. "I brought them for Fox and Hedgehog. They both said they love drumsticks."

Shrew giggled. "Good thinking, Mole," she said. "What would Thanksgiving be without drumsticks?"

A
CHRISTMAS
TALE

The Good Friends' Fur Tree

Chapter One 🐾

Outside, a baby-powder snow was falling. Inside, a fire crackled and carols played on the radio.

"Joy to the world!" sang Mole as he rolled out a batch of Christmas cookies.

Brrrinng, brrrinng! went his phone.

"Heddo, Mode," said someone when Mole answered.

"Shrew?" asked Mole. "Is that you?"

"Yeth," said Shrew, "I'm afraid I have a terrible told in my doze."

"A terrible toad!" cried Mole.

"No," said Shrew, "not a toad, a *told*. Sneezing. Sniffling…"

"Oh," said Mole, "a *cold!*"

"Yes," said Shrew, "a told."

"Poor Shrew," said Mole. "Is there anything I can do?"

"Well, dere is," said Shrew, "if you're nod too busy."

"What are friends for?" said Mole. "Of course I'm not too busy."

"Well," Shrew went on, "I haven'd godden my Chrismas tree yed, and id's Chrismas Eve. Could you ged one for me, Mode?"

"I'd be happy to," said Mole.

"Oh, thang you," said Shrew. "And, Mode, do you thing you could find a fir tree? They're my favorid."

Mole puzzled a moment. "A fur tree?" he said.

"Yes," said Shrew. "They smell so good."

"I guess it depends on the kind of fur," said Mole.

"Balsam fir is best," said Shrew.

"Right," agreed Mole. But when he hung up the phone, he was still confused. "I've never seen a tree with fur," he said to himself, "but if Shrew wants a fur tree, a fur tree she shall have."

He took his ax and headed into the forest.

Chapter Two

The snow sparkled in the sunlight as Mole trudged through the woods. He saw tall trees and short trees, wide trees and thin trees. He saw trees with stiff green needles, trees with dry brown leaves, and trees with bare branches.

But he did not see a single tree with fur.

Mole sat down on a rock.

"Umph!" said the rock.

Mole jumped up. He hadn't sat on a rock at all. He'd sat on a great old turtle.

"I beg your pardon," said Mole.

"Can I help you?" asked the turtle in a rather cross voice.

"Oh, I hope so," said Mole. "Can you tell me where I might find a fur tree?"

"Just over that ridge," said the turtle. "There's a whole grove of them."

"Oh, thank you!" cried Mole. "You've been a great help."

He ran to the top of the ridge. There before him grew hundreds of…ordinary trees.

Mole's shoulders sagged. His feet ached. The sun was sinking low and the shadows were growing long.

"I'll never find a tree for Shrew," he said.

He stared at the trees before him. Suddenly he had an idea.

"Maybe I can't *find* a fur tree," he said. "But I bet I can *make* one!"

Chapter Three

Mole chopped down a little green tree and dragged it home. Then he hurried over to Squirrel's house.

"Squirrel," he said, "may I borrow a tuft of fur?"

"A *what?*" asked Squirrel.

"A tuft of fur," Mole repeated. "I wouldn't ask, but it's for a Christmas gift, and you have such handsome fur."

"Oh," said Squirrel, puffing with pride. "I suppose a tuft of my fur *would* make a fine Christmas gift."

Squirrel pulled a small tuft from his bushy tail and handed it to Mole.

"Merry Christmas," he said.

"Merry Christmas!" Mole shouted as he hurried off.

Next Mole visited Fox's den, Hedgehog's burrow, and Rabbit's warren. When he had an armload of fur, he hurried home.

Mole hummed happily as he pasted all

the tufts onto Shrew's tree. At last it was done.

Mole beamed with pride as he loaded the tree onto his wagon.

Chapter Four

"Merry Christmas!" cried Mole when Shrew opened the door.

Shrew's eyes nearly popped out.

"Why, Mode," she said, "whad an inderesding tree!"

Mole carried the tree in and set it up in the corner.

"It's a fur tree," he said, "just the way you wanted."

"Oh...yes." Shrew's eyes twinkled

merrily. "A *fur* tree. Aren'd you a wonderful friend, Mode?"

"Yes, I am," said Mole, "only..."

"Only what, Mode?"

"I must confess," said Mole, "it isn't a balsam fur tree. We don't seem to have any balsams living in our neighborhood. It's more like a good friends' fur tree."

Shrew smiled.

"I can'd thing of a nicer kind," she said.

She stretched up to give Mole a kiss on the cheek. Then she went to the kitchen and brought back two cups of eggnog. They each took a sip, then Shrew started to giggle.

"What's so funny?" asked Mole.

"I jus thoughd of the perfecd carol for us to sing around our tree," said Shrew.

"What's that?" asked Mole.

"We Wish You a Hairy Chrismas!"
sang Shrew.

Mole laughed. Then he lifted his cup.

"A toast," he said. "To good friends at
Christmas!"

Shrew lifted her cup. "To *best* friends,"
she added, "all year through."

About
the Author

JACKIE FRENCH KOLLER wrote her first
novel when she was in the sixth grade.
She's now the author of over a dozen
books for children and lives with her
husband, three children, and two dogs in
western Massachusetts.

About
the Illustrator

JOHN BEDER is a painter and illustrator
of mythical creatures, cartoon characters,
and unlikely places. An avid reader of
metaphysics, science, and history, he can
usually be found in the company of
writers. This is his first children's book.